# HUSBANDS, WIVES AND LIVE-TOGETHERS

**Also by William Hamilton**


TERRIBLY NICE PEOPLE
WILLIAM HAMILTON'S ANTI-SOCIAL REGISTER

# HUSBANDS, WIVES AND LIVE-TOGETHERS

# WILLIAM HAMILTON

**G. P. Putnam's Sons, New York**

*To Ned Evans*

"I'm sort of para-in love."

"Actually my dad is a street person, but, you know, heh-heh, *Wall* Street."

"Dad, did you ever meet an intellectual?"

"Yes, I love you. In fact, you drive me bananas!"

"Oh, I know you *like* me—but if you *loved* me, this would be in slow motion with lots of backlighting."

"I still can't get him off my mind, even after meditating my brains out."

"'Let's go to a motel'—that's not very twenties."

"I don't think I passed. I can never remember if Robinson Crusoe is pivotal or seminal."

"Can you believe the human mind! Do you know that at this exact minute I'm thinking of amino acids, Thomas Jefferson, and you?"

"Hey, dad, take it easy! When I said I was in love with the captain of the Yale squash team, I meant the women's team."

"If only Haydn could have heard himself in quad."

"Do you have any idea what your father and I go through with each other to keep a nuclear family for you?"

"Once upon a time, long, long ago, way before everything got screwed up. . . ."

"History's sort of fun. It's about dead celebrities."

"Way long ago back then, everything was individually customized."

"Then, from the east, there came three kings, bearing gift items."

"Gosh, before long, we're going to have to come down out of the trees."

"Darling, you know you can always come home and lay your little trips on us."

"Which was really the most fun, Mr. Carmody, the twenties or the thirties?"

"Some day, Mr. Kelley, I'd like to be as old as you!"

"Oh darling, I just can't bear it that we're on different tectonic plates!"

"The most dynamite of all sacred cantatas."

"I don't believe it! Do you know I also met this bozo on a dig?"

"So I threw my needlepoint at Winslow and walked out. Now I live in a loft with a couple of guys and do stuff with steel."

"He's in the Sierra Club, but he's not, you know, a nut."

"Are you just taking pictures or are you doing photography?"

"Oh, he went to Aspen to find himself. With Sally Butterfield."

"Caviar—but I don't mean it in an elitist way."

"My love for you could withstand anything—even marriage!"

"That's just how I felt until I got these shoes that tilt you slightly back-wards."

"With all this stuff in it, it's bound to taste Chinese."

"Dues? Hey, babe, don't talk to *me* about dues. I lost 110 grand in the market."

"Meditation got me through George, but for Evan I needed a shrink."

"Ciao, and thanks, Nancy—it's such fun every so often to see main-stream friends."

"Confederate ancestors, horse racing, architecture—one more common bond and I'll scream! Did your father drink?"

"I love you, and I mean that not just personally—I mean it politically, too."

"We think we're going to go the distance."

"You know who's gotten surprisingly less wimpish? Peter Hoover!"

"You're stuffy. That's nice."

"I mean, damn it, Henry—I think I know a little bit more about our relationship than the I Ching does!"

"This is Henry. We live together, too. Only in our case, I'm afraid we're married."

"I'm getting more and more worried that what becomes of me might not happen in my own time."

"Please, Justin! Mummy is trying to structure a dinner party!"

"But, Muff, you've got to come. You fit with the Nichols."

"No one understands f.16 like Ansel Àdams!"

"Now, don't forget what I told you about Roger's need to fail."

"At last we've trashed the Stocktons!"

"I'll bet you're the neat new paddle tennis freaks Tina Barney found!"

"Phil's decided he has a sit-com in him."

"Oh, come on! You mean I'm the only one here who dropped acid at Woodstock?"

"Divine veal and we loved the graphics on the menu."

"Museum of Modern Art? Which bathroom scale is in good taste?"

"We're so excited. Tatum O'Neal is reading Evan's novel!"

"I found out why they're so incredibly laid-back: Valium."

"Bob and Gwen, I mean this terribly seriously. Seriously, we had a wonderful time. I mean that. Seriously."

"Frankly, needlepoint embodies about all I want to embody."

"I got so sick of Gucci I couldn't see straight. And now the same thing seems to be happening with Hermès."

"She's really wired in to the colonial dames."

"He keeps saying to think of utter nothingness—to empty out my mind and be one with the void. I guess I'm just not the type."

"He says we'll get married as soon as everything bounces back."

"I tried all May, June, July, and August. Then I said to hell with it and slipped back into my stereotype."

"He thinks he's so high voltage and he's really very low voltage."

"For an architect he's a very weak person."

"My problem in ceramics is never leaving well enough alone."

"He jogged into my life and jogged right back out."

"Darling! How domestic!"

"Be patient, Arch. If your parents had let you do this, you wouldn't be in analysis today."

"Completely handcarved from a single piece of whalebone by Hudson Bay Eskimos. What do you think, cigarette box or soap dish?"

"I don't know if it means anything, but I just saw three American cars in a row."

"When I suggested we 'dress thirties and go for a walk,' I didn't realize you'd come out Depressionish."

"Oh, incidentally, I found out why you don't see Jack and Sally around anymore—they went broke."

"I used every one of those cute little spice bottles."

"So far all I know is George Peppard has amnesia."

"Jack and I are chucking all our status symbols."

"Like the Louvre, our walls are hung with art, like the Baron Edmond Elie Rothschild, we drink red wine with beef, like the late Mr. Justice Holmes, I practice law, and like the late Clark Gable, I have a small mustache.

"Hi, darling—everything is in the crock pot, including yours truly."

"Darling, it's almost a year, and your marriage still isn't previous."

"No, it's not you. It's just that I'm unresponsive when I'm out of the market."

"Believe me, Peggy, I can imagine how hard this is for you—but I thought at least you'd be glad she's in Amnesty International."

"Two years ago, you said you didn't think you could live without me.
Today you left me on hold."

"I'm sick of living unpretentiously."

"You keep checking out reflections in the windows, Henry; are you looking at you or at us?"

"Gosh, Ted, has it been that long? I got over my owl thing ages ago."

"I hope this has nothing to do with my National Book Award."

"If this *were* Casablanca and you *were* Humphrey Bogart, I'd *gladly* have stuck with Paul Henreid."

"When I fell in love with you, suddenly your eyes didn't seem close together. Now they seem close together again."

"We should have invited more listeners!"

"Don't you dare! If there's table-hopping to be done, it's up to them to make the first hop."

"I almost died over your pronunciation of 'oeuvre.'"

"I did not say 'shut up'—I simply said 'clam it.'"

"And my husband isn't the *only* one who doesn't understand me."

"I suppose I should have expected it: marry a jock, and you wind up with a former jock."

"To think how when I couldn't sleep I'd write you sonnets!"

"To hell with you *and* your guidelines!"

"Technically, I do love you."

"Let's face it—you were my dues and I was your dues."

"All right, ciao, but I want you to know, this is one of the hardest ciaos I've ever had to say."

"Remember how I told you my head was in a new place? I've decided to put the rest of me there, too."

"Richard! That jogger! It's my husband!"

"I'm sick of you, Henry. I'm sick of you, and I'm sick of denim!"

"I gave some money to a beggar today."

"Here, and pay attention. It was $11.99."

"It's an awful feeling, as though there will never be anything more to add to my résumé."

"Oh, no! An unresolvable conflict between *Gourmet* and Julia!"

"Remember when we used to take those Italian movie-style walks together?"

"I've had all my minimum daily adult requirements, except bourbon."

"Of all the deals I ever made, Nanny-Poo, you were one of the smartest."

"Bobby, I want a mood ring—an emerald."

"Please, Diane. Get a good night's sleep, and rethink me in the morning."

"Phoebe, all I want to do is normalize our relations."

"I wanted to be an American novelist. American is as far as I got."

"I thought I saw William Holden yesterday, but it was just a William Holden look-alike."

"So you're Andrew Rogers! You were on my first husband's Rolodex."

"They were relatively nice men, Caroline. What do you suppose turned them into oenophiles?"

"She's neat, but he's marginal."

"Excuse me, Nancy—this isn't the one incapable of sustaining personal relationships, is it?"

"Oh, you'll *adore* them. They're from France and they have lots of—you know, money."

"It turns out their pied-à-terre is all they have."

"Oh, dear, I was afraid we'd meet you. We've been waiting for you to come out in paperback."

"You never heard Thomas Jefferson apologize for being a wealthy liberal."

"Oh, yes, we know them. We hate them."

"And now: a double digit Bordeaux!"

"I'd heard you'd remarried, but I had no idea it was to my first wife."

"It's so rare to meet someone who actually still is a spring chicken!"

"Ciao, Joan. That was an incredibly together duck."

"Now please don't try to fill the room with your presence."

"The Kingsleys were not my idea, they were your idea. Jerry Bestor was my idea."

"To think how I used to worry about you and Larry back before you were married, doing whatever it was you did in that little van."

"Give it to me straight, Marnie—do I have greedy little pig eyes?"

"Does helping with the dishes mean you've started another little love affair?"

"Did you ever stop to think about the raw data I've got on you?"

"I understand your affair with the wines of the Médoc isn't the only affair you're having."

"Harry, is finding the best chocolate ice cream going to make us better people?"

"How many times do I have to tell you to stay the hell away from me when I'm writing poetry!"

"I'm sorry, George. I ran a projection on you."

"Maybe it's not New York. Maybe it's you."

"Do you call that an answer, Margaret, 'none of your beeswax'?"

"First we were an extended family, then we were a nuclear family, and now we're divorced."

"Let's face it, Doris. This marriage is Chapter XI!"

"No, Charles, I don't have a cold. What you hear in my voice is contempt."

"What is it this time? My maleness? My Anglo-Saxonness? My Prince-tonness? My lawyerness?"

"Tell me, Charlie—anything in those indicators of yours about a divorce?"

"The only thing about you that ever matured is your bonds."

"And another thing, Margo. I'm sick of supplying all the input in these arguments."

"You mean I'm a lie, l-i-e eating your guts out, or a lye, l-y-e eating your guts out?"

"My wife just pulled an Anna Karenina on me."

"Do you realize what the promotion means—it means at last we can afford a divorce!"

"Let's face it, Harold. We've reached the saturation point."

"Why try to bail ourselves out? Why not just bail out?"

"Now the first change we recommend is your name. I'm sure you all agree 'The People's Transportation Collective' has it all over 'General Motors.'"

"I'm seriously thinking of getting three new younger, brighter idiots."

"I peaked too soon."

"It seems like only yesterday, and actually it was millions and millions of dollars ago."

"Steel, of course, has been my life. But sometimes I wish my life had
been sitting with a pretty girl in a sunny café in Provence, drinking
Beaujolais."

"See, Johnny? Really good California wine is just like really good French wine."

"If we're going to communicate, Margaret, you're going to have to quantify."

"I'm in publishing, Jeff, because I love language and money talks!"

"I made the broad on our board of directors cry."

"Let's face it—we need not only a very creative lawyer, we need a very
slick lawyer."

"You've got people skills—you fire him."

"Gee, that's too bad. You know, the wife's brother also got zapped. Only he didn't get zapped in wheat futures, he got zapped in cocoa."

"I like the way you push, Dodds. Pushers eventually become movers and shakers."

"I always knew what I wanted, and I always knew how I wanted it: hand over fist!"

"Lately you never seem to come down from the corporate level."

"I'm not feeling very well, Emma. Keep the younger executives at bay."

"Now, Ackley, come to bed—it wasn't *you* they rejected, it was just your weapons system."

"It was Grampa Higgins, God bless him, who started the company. No, wait a minute, it was Grampa Pearson, God bless him, who started the company. Grampa Higgins, God bless him, started the bank."

"As my late husband used to say—or was it you, Willis. . . ."

"Now, Eric—remember you promised last year not to let not getting the Nobel Prize bother you again this year."

"Francis, do you believe in make-believe?"

"The pressure comes from my public and, of course, my editors and agents and producers and all that—but the real pressure comes from that devil inside that makes me different from other men, that makes me a writer. But of course you know all about pressure—having to pass those exams out at Sarah Lawrence."

"Tell me about your ascent."

"It's always been you, kid—before, during, and after my mustache."

"Well, as I said it would a million years ago, it all came out in the wash: me losing your inheritance, your little affair with Sam Winchester. . . ."

"The senior prom, the summer in Maine, the honeymoon in Europe—
God, Marla, if only it had been *you* instead of Phoebe Henshaw!"

# Our Neglected Rich

Like a school of fish or a flight of birds that mysteriously change direction in unison at an untraceable psychic drill command, our journalists have deserted the rich and now devote their attentions to the poor. In plump times there is only rarely and self-consciously a little piece about the poor over which we rush with a genteel shudder as we look for the feature story on Mimi Powerbucks' life-style. But as soon as Mr. Recession comes to call, every typewriter ribbon in town is bludgeoned with chilling interviews with the jobless.

It's simply that in rich times the rich set the style and in poor times the poor set the style. Recently a fashion magazine had lavish photographs of what it assured us was the fun new thing, the austere dinner party. The photographs showed more plate than chow, and a particularly heartless white Japanese porcelain plate at that. The rich are looking for jobs now—a thing they would never do if there were jobs enough for everyone—because, being fashion-conscious, they sense how very now job hunting has become.

"No one cares about us" is a complaint you hear more and more in the marble and gilt of the nation's salons.

"Lots of people think the worst is yet to come," a racehorse owner confided to us as he gazed ruefully at the Jockey Club Gold Cup filled with cymbidium on his Marie Antoinette (signed) escritoire. "If it keeps up, I don't know what we're going to do. My wife took two years to decorate our new apartment and we can't even get photographs into my hometown newspaper."

There has always been a native optimism in America, and that spirit endures, even among the rich in hard times. Able to pooh-pooh negativism no matter how heavy the weather, sorts like these are an inspiration in a time when so few can see above the Dow. But some, under a brave facade, are obviously churning inside.

## C. WHITEMAN BURDEN,
**Diplomat, philanthropist, art collector, bibliophile, Légion d'honneur, Society of the Cincinnati, turf figure**

"What our citizens need is a sense of history," affirms Mr. Burden, who is in many ways a piece of living history himself. "With the long and generous view of the historical perspective, the peculiar eccentricities of the moment become much less significant. I strongly advocate giving the jobless texts describing the founding of our great nation. What better time to get our people into the great panorama of our past than now? A good scholar is a hungry scholar and that requirement is generously filled by this present insignificant drop in the great bucket of American history. The unemployed and the underfed would both be better off in a library than whining in the streets, which, by the way, are utterly filthy.

"As for how we got into this mess, I would just like to point out that my own present comfort, financial comfort, is the result of a very simple, basic economic rule that would have kept every American out of financial straits had they stuck to it. The rule is: Don't dip into capital. Spend only income. Except for my great-aunt Hattie in Paris in '78, no member of my family has touched capital since 1697, when Isaak Burden made it a rule to be followed. None of us has regretted our ancestor's sage advice, and I offer it up freely to the American people of today who, no matter how unattractive, are, after all, the heirs of our forefathers."

## MAISIE GRACE,
### Heiress

"There's just no fun around!" ejaculated Maisie as she flung her little Porthault hankie at Jack the cat, who sprang off the pillow Maisie had needlepointed herself (or anyway got started) of one of those Roy Lichtenstein scenes from a comic book. She picked up the hankie and wiped off her angry tear and looked at herself in the mirror.

"I have all the most divine thirties things, and nobody's in the mood because they all went down the tubes. I hate Arabs, and that's all there is. Arabs, Arabs, Arabs. Did you know El Morocco is an Arab name?

"You know, I have all my favorite recipes ready so when they interview me I can tell them, and nobody interviews me to find out my favorite recipes even. I have a list of where I shop and what I think is fun and who I admire in history, Bette Davis and Catherine the Great by the way, and what's it all for?

"When you go shopping, you know what the signs say? Liquidation! That's not a very nice thing to hear! Every place is the same. London and Paris are awful. I think this is a time to be private. To have private parties and visit people at their private homes and boats and things. Nobody's left in my exercise class or my meditation group except the creepy teachers. No wonder they call these things depressions!"

## JACK MOREJACK
### The Golden Golfer

Spring has arrived and Jack is in his famous "charge" on the mark of $300,000 by Labor Day that was set on last year's tour by none other than Jack himself.

"It's a way to psych yourself up," explained the easygoing, twenty-six-year-old star of the links. "You need pressure parameters to keep your game in focus. I was mainly just concentrating on getting to the green, and it was a big surprise to me when I realized I'd already banked two hundred thousand dollars by Washington's Birthday. That's when I knew to keep championship form I was going to have to go for the big one, the big three with the five zeroes, you know, to keep interested in my game."

Jack's reading of our current economic woes draws on his travels to nearly every state in the Union, picking up purses.

"I think the country is sort of like golf," he mused. "When your game's off, the best thing to do is just take a little time off and go fishing or something, so you can come back fresh. Who wants to be one of those poor saps that lose their confidence and can't make the cut and fall off the tour and drink themselves to death as assistant pro at some little loser country club in the middle of nowhere? That's not going to happen to me, and it's not going to happen to this country. This is a great country. This country has more than twenty two-hundred-thousand-dollar golf tournaments!"

## MOORE N. MOORE
### Tycoon

The truth of M. N. Moore lies somewhere between the harsh estimate his competitors give him ("ruthless," "heartless," "inhuman") and that of his highest-echelon employees ("sagacious," "canny," "demanding"). One of the few men actually to sharpen his profit curve as others helplessly honed their loss curves, Mr. Moore has always looked on failure as the failed's own fault. With the chuckle that twice tripped fatal coronaries in those who fought him in boardrooms, Moore expresses none of the pessimism so many money men exude.

"If they're not getting any juice, it's because they just don't know how to squeeze this lemon.

"Gee, I don't know what all the grousing is about. If it's so hard to make money now, how come I'm making so much? I think it's time for America to quit moaning and do what it's being paid to do or go look for a job someplace else!

"When I kicked all the deadheads out of CT&D [Climax Tool and Die], they howled I was a pirate and a raider. But all I did was sell everything salable, fire everything expendable, and squeeze profit out of what was left. That's what capitalism is supposed to be for, at least the way I learned it, and I am a capitalist."

## TOMMY COMMONTOUCH
### Entertainer

"Listen, baby, unemployment is box-office!" explained Tommy Commontouch at his spectacular fiscal-new-year party in Beverly Hills. Celebrities from every walk of show biz, their families, and their retinues jammed the marble and gilt acres of Tommy's superlavish mansion (Tommy bought the residences of Rudolph Valentino, Greta Garbo, and William Randolph Hearst and had them dismantled and reassembled as one colossal unit).

"Look at us," said genial Tommy, waving a freckled country-boy hand ablaze with gems and gold, "crooners, comedians, quarterbacks, and good old-fashioned movie stars—we never had it so good!"

The startlingly familiar faces of Tommy's guests laughed over globes of great French champagne and pungent Asian reefers. Anchormen, tight ends, forwards, talk-show kingpins—all the gilded personalities of an age that gilds its personalities were there.

"The right-on thing about us millionaire celebrities," philosophized Tommy, "is folks like us. I mean folks didn't like J. P. Morgan and Cornelius Vanderbilt and John D. Rockefeller. But for some reason they still like us. I like to think it's not our money; I like to think folks just like us for ourselves."

# SANTA'S LIST
## (BOOKS DIVISION)

Come Christmas, come books! Easy to wrap, complimenting the intellect as they complement the wallpaper, books have been great gift items for centuries!

These days, a book is more than just a little package of information. Books have become chunks of the author's karma, and media penetration brings us the author along with the book. Peeping out of TV and print interviews, the author has become an almost palpable presence—an aura, if you're into that—attached to the volume you pick up at your bookstore.

With this in mind, we're offering a very new, very now kind of selection to help you sift through this fall's list of books.

We're showing you the back cover—a picture of the author—and providing a brief sketch of the person whose aura you or a loved one will be dealing with. Our idea is to spare you some of those dust-jacket disasters you may have experienced in the past (the baleful stare of a loser, the assault of extreme ugliness, or the shock of an obscene gesture).

We know our authors, and just as we guarantee their competence in TV interviews, we guarantee *you* the comfort of being sure you haven't purchased the work of a person likely to track bad press into your or your giftee's library. If yours is the kind of sensitivity that prompts you to feel you're making a home for author as well as book, this list is for you. Remember—every message brings a messenger!

## "HOW TO PUT DOWN DESPAIR AND GROOVE ON LOVE"

### THE BROLLNERS

The Brollners insist their how-to book was an absolutely communal effort that had input even from their old English sheepdog, Winnie. Zack, Maria (pronounced Mareye-a), and young Adam came to their revolutionary insights the hard way. Analysis, divorce, alcohol, drugs, encounter, group sex, primal scream, adultery, embezzlement, Buddhism, and Ibiza are only some of the elemental forces shaping them.

Their collaboration, both on the book and on the many interviews and other promotional gigs marking its publication, have put them, in their words, "very, very together." Surprisingly, none of the Brollners is related. They discovered they all had the same name while they were standing in an unemployment-insurance line. What else they discovered makes very cool, high-energy reading.

## "TIMBERRR!"

### OLE DOOLEY

*Timberrr!* makes as good reading as Ole makes good looking! We've selected it from this year's disaster offerings because, besides the big-cataclysm feeling, it has an ecological feeling. The plot centers on the felling of California's largest sequoia, the General Sherman. It's a red-blooded work about a tough chain-saw man who sees a lot more go down the river than trees.

We needn't say much about Ole, because his picture is surely worth a thousand words. He was picked over both Charton Heston and Burt Reynolds to play the lead in the film version of this woodland epic.


## "DR. WATSON'S COOK, LOSE WEIGHT, AND MAKE LOVE AT THE SAME TIME BOOK"

### DR. WALDO WATSON, D.V.M.

You'll be pleased to know the doctor's voice is as avuncular, bookish, and old-cardiganish as his picture. His screen test was positive. He even came across with a sort of fatherly quality—a bonanza plus for a scribe in this medium.

As for the work itself, just the list of unexpected uses for twelve items found in every kitchen is enough to outdistance the competition.

You can look for the good doctor in chats with both Johnny Carson and Merv Griffin this winter, and should his book do a million in North American sales, Dr. Watson will throw out the first ball for the Oakland A's next season.

### "THE FOXCLIFFE TONTINE"

### SAMANTHA WAKEFIELD QUARTERPOLE

    Ms. Quarterpole's dreamy voice and lilting, genteel Virginia accent make the content of whatever she says secondary. On TV, she will make you feel you and she are alone on a veranda long ago and far away.

    Her novel follows the careers of the illegitimate line of the Duke from her last opus, *Candlewycke.* Just the thing to make time fly for sunbathers, invalids, and *au pairs.*

    Ms. Quarterpole's legs are sensational!

### "GENERAL GEORGE WASHINGTON:
### AN AMERICAN LIFE"

### J. C. HIGGINS

    Like the volumes he pens, Mr. Higgins is beautifully bound. His tailor has adroitly matched the impeccable speech and meticulous—but not finicky—mannerisms of his patron. Mr. Higgins speaks—in addition to English—French. He was educated completely in private schools.

    The book itself is a thing of beauty. A truly historical-looking item, emblazoned with eagles, drums, stars, muskets, and other appropriate symbols.

## TOMORROW'S CELEBRITIES TODAY

    One of the few fields still expanding despite the blasts and pestilences of the current economy is Celebrity. Once a phenomenon restricted to such exclusive vocations as crowned head, field marshal, and assassin, Celebrity has exploded to include such down-to-earth occupations as quarterback, anchorman, and hooker.

The marvel of television is largely responsible for the Cinderella-like transformations achieved by many formerly unheralded occupations. With slow motion to provide grace to the clumsiest gesture, instant replay to reexamine what Marcel Proust knew only as *temps perdu,* as well as laugh tracks and the rest of TV's magic, almost anyone can entertain us.

And yet millions of Americans still go to bed at night obscure. One reason is that most people pursue fame in the most difficult and unimaginative way. Rather than attempt to be something you're not, be it rock musician, pop writer, or simply divine-looking, why not consider seeking fame in less competitive fields?

To extrapolate from the quantum spread of Celebrity over the recent past, it's safe to guess that many currently banal activities will soon be avenues to star (or even superstar) dom.

Here are capsule bios of some clever people who have already staked claims in what may be tomorrow's Celebrity Bonanza.

## DEBBIE DARE

From the age of six, through piano lessons, elocution lessons, dance, makeup, and singing lessons, Debbie Dare has been trying to break into show business. Her three marriages to lying deadbeats claiming to be entertainment biggies, her countless hours waiting for the "big chance" (Debbie holds waiting-room records at Warners, Fox, and MCA), and the heartbreak of the aging process led Debbie to consider early retirement. Then one day inspiration struck, and success was almost immediate.

"I was in an elevator that was playing 'It's Only a Paper Moon' when I got the idea for what I now call the Public Recording Field. I pressed the button for the executive offices, and the very next week I was the voice of the floors at Macy's! From there it was a short step to supermarket specials, political-campaign trucks, and time zones. I've done both the Mountain and Pacific Standard time zones. (I think everybody in the business ought to do an occasional gig on the Coast.)

"I've also done some Off Broadway—you know, the 'Please stand back from the moving platform' in the IRT down on Fourteenth Street—some weather in Central Park (without word one from Joseph Papp, by the way), and some spiritual things for Dial-A-Prayer.

"Really, there's been so much work I've decided to get out of town with my plants and cat, put my feet up, and just take a rest. But," she added with a twinkle in her eye, "I'm taking a briefcase full of scripts with me."

## ERNIE NAVONI

"To get famous today," says Ernie Navoni, "you got to deal with women. Look at your barbers, look at your tailors. The most they can get is successful. But your hairdressers and your fashion designers, they get *famous.* The reason is they deal with women, and women like to read about and deal with celebrities, so they make the people they buy from famous. And who deals with women who isn't famous yet? Butchers.

"When a butcher sharpens a big knife, an electric current runs through the ladies. The conversation is hot stuff, and I don't mean just oven temperatures. Butchers routinely discuss such sensual items as taste and tenderness. Now you can't tell me a man with a nice pair of forearms and big slabs of naked meat hanging all around him is not a sex object! Ask your psychiatrist. Butchers are ready for the big time, the talk shows, the as-told-tos, throwing out the first ball—the whole side of beef.

"The question is: How do I elevate meat from a comestible to a status symbol? How do I make meat chic? Answer: I do just what the footwear and handbag guys did. I personalize meat! The trick is distinctive stripes, and my initials applied in such a manner that they won't cook off in the oven. Now the lady can lay out a dish that everyone recognizes as an Ernie Navoni. Mark my words. By the end of the year, people will be complimenting the hostess by saying, 'My dear, I *loved* your Ernie Navoni.'"

## THE DRUGSTORE

Six months ago, Norm Stockton, Ken Childs, and Ned Bevens were three unkindled rock stars watching the sunset of their youth take place behind the mountain of anonymity. Unskilled beyond the rudimentary musical and electronic know-how required by their trade, they faced an uncertain future. But things have changed for the trio. They've moved out of the overtraveled rock rut and into a new groove, which seems destined to lead them to a different kind of stardom.

Norm, Ken, and Ned, formerly known as Vortex, The Megatons, Summer Trip, and Mold, have sold off their Fenders, Gibsons, and platform shoes and enrolled at pharmacology school!

"One day, we were kicking around some new names for the group," Ken explained, "and Ned came up with The Drugstore. Then Norm says, 'Hey, wait a minute! Why don't we really *do* a drugstore?'"

"I got this great flash!" Norm added. "A kind of head-shop-style drugstore that kids can get next to. A whole chain, with these wiggy pharmacists in sequined white pharmacist outfits, who, like, laugh insanely while they prepare your prescription. I mean, the kids will freak out. And Ned and Ken and me, we image the thing. We do the appearances, like Vegas and the talk-show trip, and franchise the whole insane number."

"Can you dig it?" enthused Ken. "See, the current heavies of drugstore franchising, they got your Geritol crowd, which is cool with us, because, like, we're going after the kids. See where I'm coming from? They can have the crowd getting old now, because we will have the crowd that is going to get old in the future. It's like Walgreen's and Rexall are the Mills Brothers of pharmaceuticals and we are the Rolling Stones."

## CAL CROCKER

Ten years of scrounging for bit parts and food in southern California persuaded Cal Crocker to try an area less crowded with charisma than the one covered by *Variety*. Cal has traded the cattle calls of casting for the archetypal cattle calls of actual cattle. Although yet to land his first part in agriculture, Cal is enthusiastic about getting in at the beginning of an industry he believes will soon be as big as film, recording, and pro sports.

"The Russian wheat deal is typical of the agricultural spectaculars coming down on viewers!" exclaimed Cal as he tried on his new denim overalls. "I like the costumes and the organic angle. And between appearances you've got the basic gig of farming to keep body and tan together."